D1545240

A DIFFERENT VIEW:
A Story of Friendship and Discovery

Written by Romana Hasnain

Illustrated by Elizabeth Zwolski

A Different View: A Story of Friendship and Discovery

by Romana Hasnain

Copyright © 2014 by MR KAZ Publishing
Chicago, IL

All rights reserved.

This book is protected under the copyright laws of the United States of America. Any reproduction or other unauthorized use of the material or artwork herein is prohibited without the express written permission of the author.

Just outside the pretty French village of Yvoire, a sunflower and a wood mouse strike up an unusual friendship in this gloriously illustrated children's book. Go along for the adventure as Florette and Vincent realize the power of working together, and each discovers a magical different view of the world. A great read-to book for ages 2-6, with a story and illustrations that older kids will enjoy too.

ISBN: 978-0-9964191-0-9

LCCN: 2015909502
MR KAZ Publishing, Chicago IL.

To my three adventurers,
Kavon, Aiden, and Zan.
-Romana

To Mom for putting the crayon in
my hand and to Dad for telling me
to shoot for the moon.
-Elizabeth

Each morning, sunflowers around the world raise their faces east to greet the rising sun.

They hold their faces high to the sky the whole day through.

As the sun sets in the west, sunflowers bow their yellow crowned heads.

By the time darkness falls, they are asleep.

But in a sunflower field outside the pretty French village of Yvoire, nestled by the French Alps, a young sunflower named Florette questioned this convention. "What is this mysterious time called night?" she asked the other sunflowers.

None of them had seen night.

She decided she would **not** fall asleep that night.
Thinking about seeing night made her nervous but excited.
She felt a tingling up her stem.

The next day, Florette woke with the rising sun, but when the sun began to set, she refused to bow her head.

Soon, her eyes began to feel heavy.

The further the sun set, the heavier they became.

Before the sun had set completely, Florette was fast asleep.

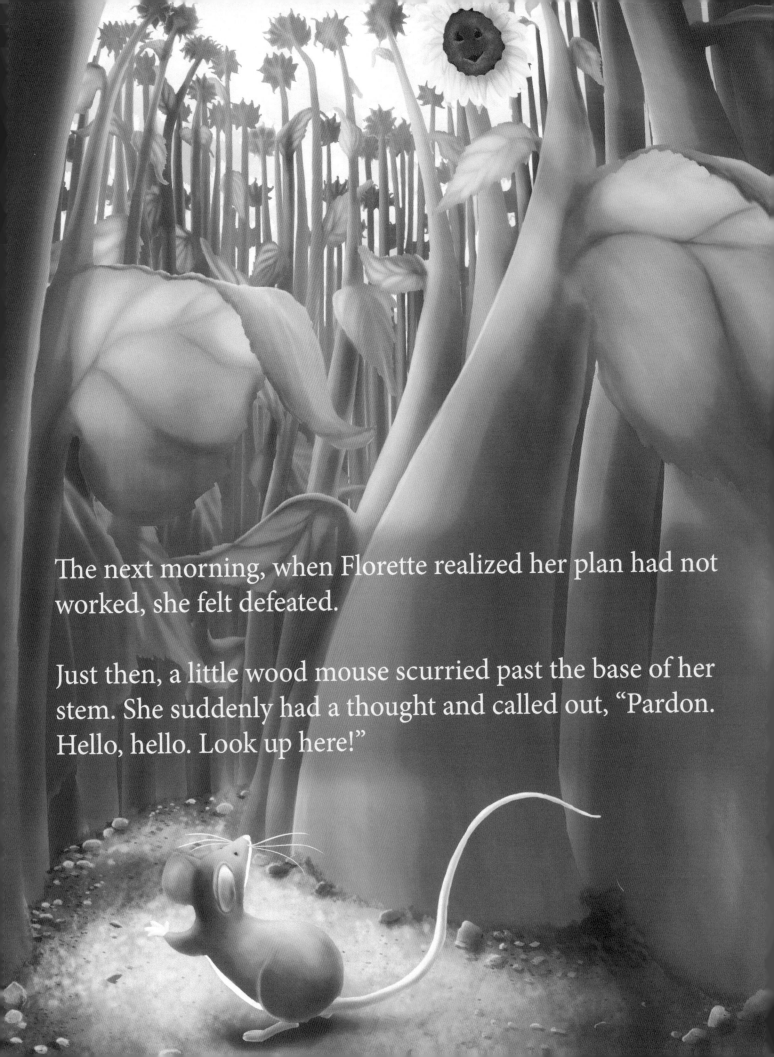

The next morning, when Florette realized her plan had not worked, she felt defeated.

Just then, a little wood mouse scurried past the base of her stem. She suddenly had a thought and called out, "Pardon. Hello, hello. Look up here!"

The little wood mouse startled and looked up. Florette smiled, "Bonjour, my name is Florette. How are you?"

He replied in a hesitant tone, "I'm fine, thank you. I've never had a sunflower speak to me before."

Florette looked at the tiny creature with its big eyes and ears. "What is your name?" she asked.

"Vincent," he replied.

"Nice to meet you, Vincent. I was wondering if you could answer a question for me."

Vincent felt honored and BIG to think that he could help this tall sunflower.

"I'll try," he replied.

"Well, I was wondering," said Florette softly, "have you ever been awake at night?"

"Yes, of course, that is when I forage for food," said Vincent.

Florette said somewhat sadly, "Well, I have never seen night.

When I tried to stay awake, I couldn't."

Vincent listened.

"Well," he said, "I've never seen anything but the ground in this sunflower field.

It's cool down here, and it's safe because owls can't see us.

But, I don't know what it feels like to be directly in the sun's warmth, or what the view is like from high off the ground."

Florette listened.

Then, in an eager voice, she said, "You know, we can help each other!"

"If you climb up to my top leaf, you can help me stay awake at night, and I will help you see the view and feel the warmth of the sun during the day!"

Vincent had never felt so excited, "What a brilliant idea!" he exclaimed.

"Let's both rest up and I will come back tomorrow before sunset."

Florette smiled and nodded, "Perfect!"

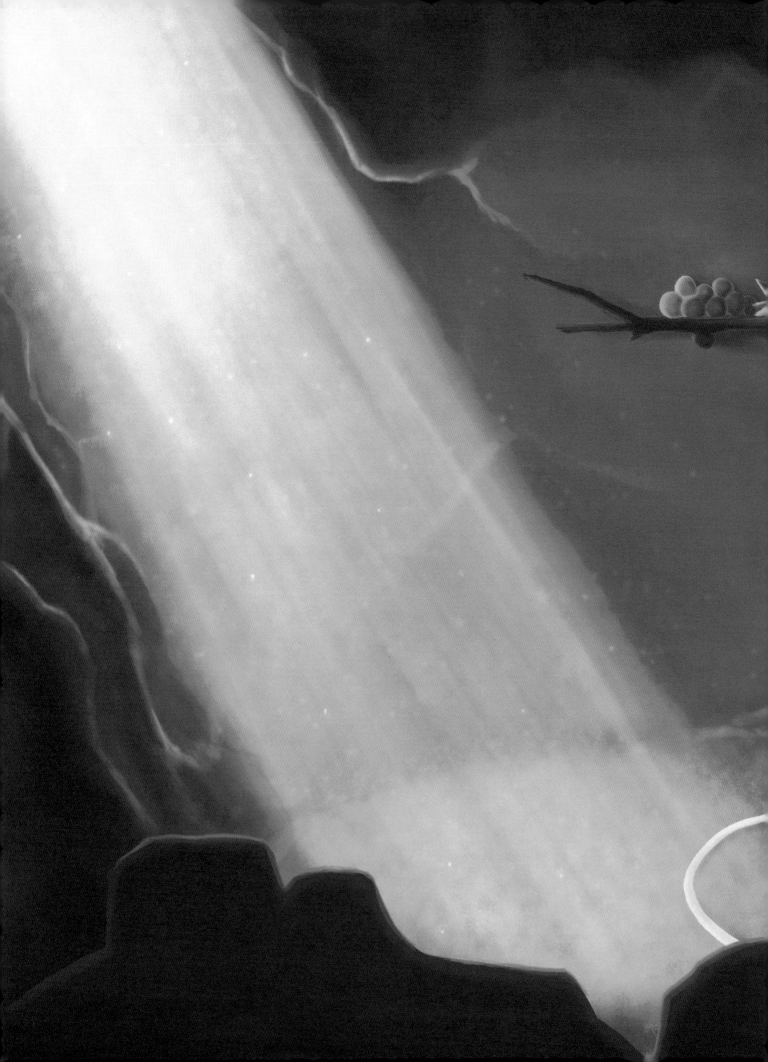

Vincent went home to his burrow to rest. He couldn't believe how his life had just changed.

He was going to help a sunflower realize her dream, and make his own dream come true, too.

Florette was having similar thoughts.

As the sun began to set that evening, her head grew heavy.

She readily lowered it and went into a deep sleep in anticipation of the next night.

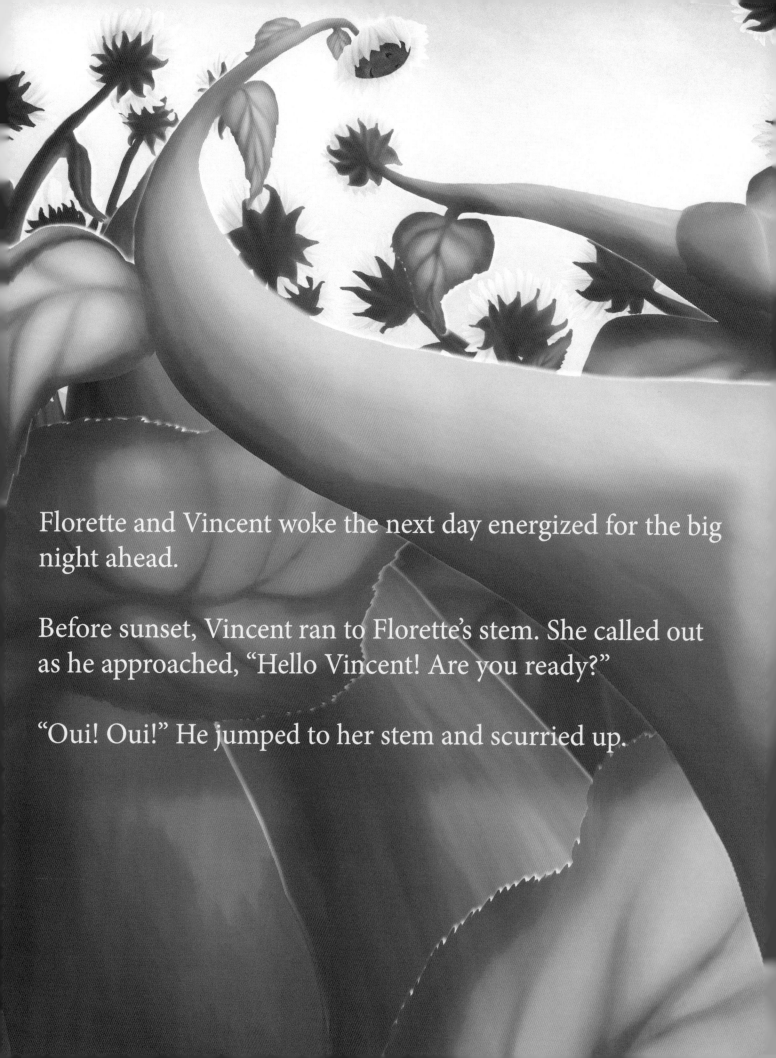

Florette and Vincent woke the next day energized for the big
night ahead.

Before sunset, Vincent ran to Florette's stem. She called out
as he approached, "Hello Vincent! Are you ready?"

"Oui! Oui!" He jumped to her stem and scurried up.

Vincent climbed onto the highest leaf next to Florette's crown of petals. The sun was beginning to set over the horizon, and Florette could already feel the pull of sleep.

Vincent told her rousing stories about his adventures. Florette looked at the little wood mouse with his long tail, brown head, and white torso.

She smiled.

It seemed just minutes later when, laughing at one of Vincent's stories, she realized the sun had disappeared.

Her eyes began to adjust to the darkness and she saw that the sky was sparkling!

Florette gasped, "Look at all the shiny things in the sky! I feel like I can almost touch the glowing ball."

Suddenly, Vincent trembled as he heard flapping feathers.

A large tawny owl flew toward them.

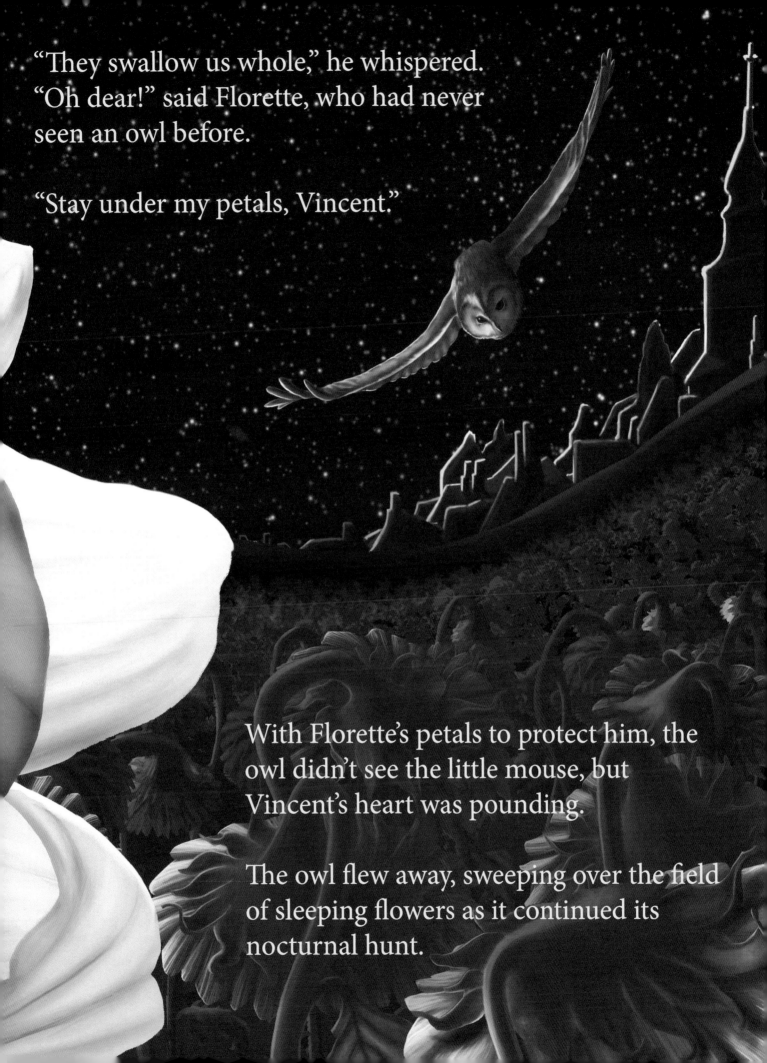

"They swallow us whole," he whispered.
"Oh dear!" said Florette, who had never
seen an owl before.

"Stay under my petals, Vincent."

With Florette's petals to protect him, the
owl didn't see the little mouse, but
Vincent's heart was pounding.

The owl flew away, sweeping over the field
of sleeping flowers as it continued its
nocturnal hunt.

Florette was amazed by the sights and smells and cool feel of night. She shared her awe with Vincent and sighed, "What a marvelous view."

The excitement of their adventure had caught up with them. Soon they were both asleep.

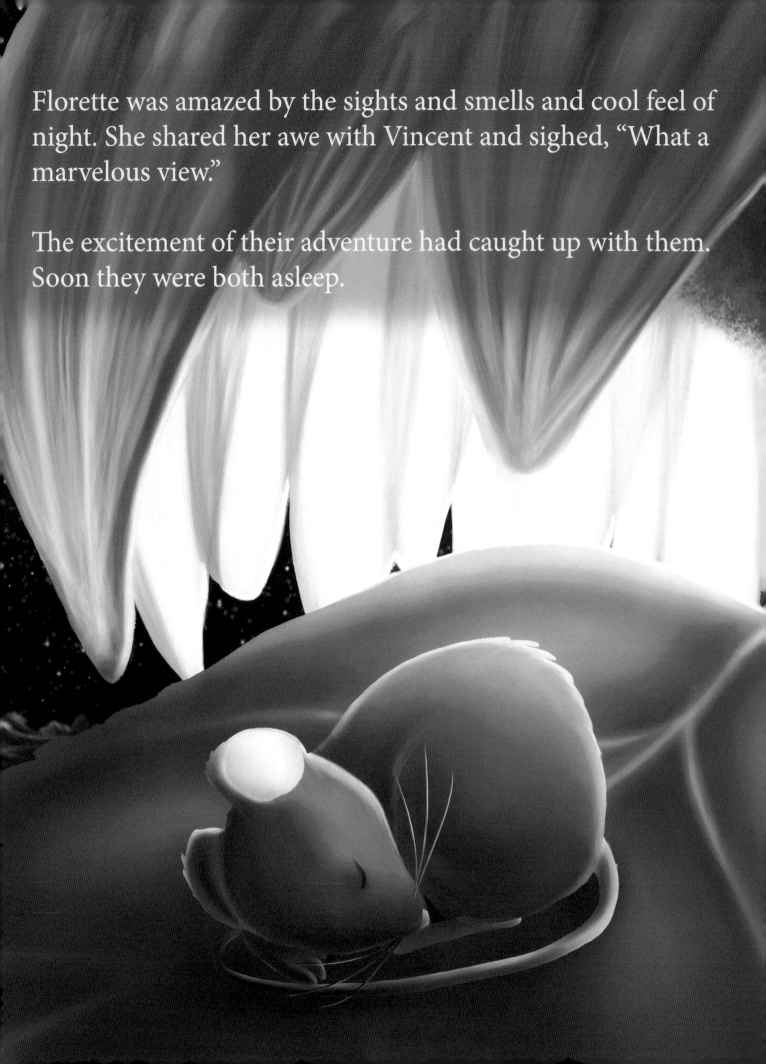

The next morning, as the sun rose in the east, Florette woke up and started to lift her head toward the rising sun.

She saw Vincent fast asleep. "Wake up," she whispered. "The sun is rising."

Vincent opened his eyes and looked toward the sun coming up over the horizon. He had never seen such a beautiful sight in his life.

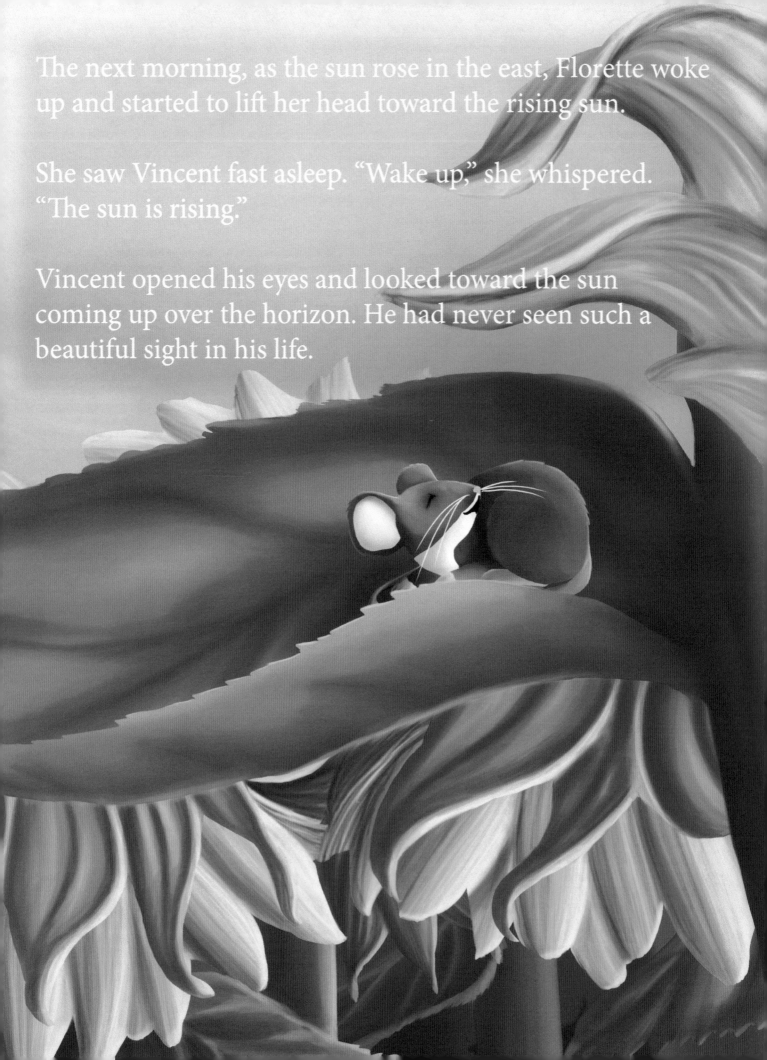

It was his turn
to be amazed.

He basked in the warmth of the sun as it washed the field in its morning light. "What a marvelous view!"

From Florette's top leaf he felt tall and brave. "Thank you, Florette!" he said.

Florette felt proud and grateful too. She was the first sunflower ever to see the night sky, and she had made a best friend.

Florette and Vincent looked at each other, smiled, and at the same time whispered, "Marvelous!"

About the Author

Romana Hasnain is the mother of three sons, with whom she has shared many adventures, including some in Yvoire, France. She lives in Chicago and Colorado, writing and growing sunflowers and other flora.
romanahasnain1@ gmail.com

About the Illustrator

Elizabeth (Beth) Zwolski has been drawing ever since her mom first placed a crayon in her hand. She graduated from Columbia College Chicago and has been building a gallery of mixed art. http://www.ezwolski.com